WRITE
OUT
OF
MY
MIND

BY MARTIN POVEY

A PREMIUM COLLECTION
PAIRING PHOTOGRAPHS, POETRY & PROSE

1

Lust or love? Is there a difference?

Can killing be humorous?

What do dead fish and Greek gods have in common?

This premium collection of verse and versatile short stories serves up the answers in this dim sum for the mind.

Served up in delicious bite-sized treats, this compelling collection will tempt every taste. And to satisfy the eyes, each work is accompanied by the photography that inspired its writing!

Write Out of My Mind is guaranteed to produce a smile, prompt a tear or two and perhaps even change the way you think and feel.

This one is dedicated to my wife and life partner
Mary Lou.

She knows all the reasons why.

To me, words are my adult surrogate for the Lego set I had growing up.

Join the individual pieces together, one by one, and those individual pieces turn into something else.

A sentence.

Take these unified pieces; join them to each other and presto!

A paragraph.

It's easy to make the mistake of thinking that imagination is like inspiration—that it just kind of happens. Not true. Imagination is just like a muscle—it will become weaker or stronger depending on how it is fed and used.

So, words are one form of expressing what lurks hidden away in your imagination and, if you exercise it, then pretty soon plucked from your imagination, just like that Lego space station or magical forest from childhood, there's a short story, a book, a poem, a play, a script and so on and so on.

Words. Strung together in harmony. They explain a feeling, convey a compelling message, or, communicate a concept. Words can provide fleeting gratification, or, make you stop and think; they can stimulate the spirit, stir the soul and move the mind. For a moment, or, forever.

Damn – I love words.

Sunday Bloody Sunday

I saw it from a bus and just knew I had to write something about it. I was on a field trip, a writer's version of prospecting for gold, when I found this nugget. I just had to come up with an idea for the framework around it. Some 6 months later it all came together and is now, one of my all-time favourites. I hope you enjoy it too!

Sunday Bloody Sunday

The man with the carefully groomed Jesus beard shuffled down the shady side of the street. He ducked to avoid the faded awning of the coffee shop and stopped.

A grubby Billy Joel T-shirt hung loosely over worn down camouflage pants which could no longer hide months of soils and stains.

His T-shirt said The Piano Man Tour 19 Something, but like much of his life the date had been obliterated.

He slouched against the grimy window, scanning the street like a hawk seeking its next meal.

He found his prey.

Three doors down, a woman wearing a fire engine red dress thrust a cigarette between matching red lips.

He'd seen her before. She worked the street maybe. Didn't she know it was Sunday, the day of rest?

How'd it get to be Sunday again. He mused. Not that he worked the other 6 days anyway. God knows, every day was a day of rest for him, he thought bitterly.

He'd had an ongoing, one sided argument with God ever since his last tour of duty in Croatia.

Croatia. God in heaven might have forgotten about that place. But he sure remembered that hell on earth.

He could still smell the salty sweet sweat of the young girl in the bombed out village as he'd swept her up into his arms.

He could still see the 'everything's going to be OK isn't it' look of hope and trust in her eyes.

Except it hadn't been OK.

Before she'd died she'd had whispered final words in a language he'd never understand and one he'd never hear again.

During the next explosion God took the young girl away.

God and the explosion also took away his hearing.

Some lovin' God, he thought.

He figured red dress was a easy mark.

He sauntered down to her.

"Bumma smoke?"

She said nothing. Just handed him the pack.

"Bumma light?"

She sighed, blew smoke in his face and swapped him her lighter for the pack.

"You have yourself a nice day ma'am," he thanked her and began to move away.

"Hey, my lighter" came her sharp voice.

He just smiled.

"My lighter, gimme my lighter back," snatching it from his hand.

He smiled again, just nodded.

He turned away, his attention caught by a young couple, arms wrapped around each other.

They'd stopped at an alleyway further down the block.

She pointed, tossed back her long dark hair laughing. Heads together and giggling the secrets that only young lovers can, they moved on.

Curious now, he loped on down to the alleyway and saw what had so amused the young couple.

Throwing what was left of his cigarette into the street, the man walked slowly across the cracked concrete, drawn to it like an old lover to a past affair.

Holy shee-it, he thought unbelievingly.

He reached out, sighing wistfully as he stroked the sun splintered top.

He leaned over and hesitantly opened the piano's blistered rotten lid and sighed again.

Back on the street, a rusting dark green pick-up truck back-fired as it skidded to an unplanned stop at a crosswalk.

A group of kids screamed and shouted as they ran across the street in front of it.

The pick-up backfired again as it revved up and took off.

The man who'd heard none of this reached out gently, tentatively, stroking, caressing the battered keys with long nicotine stained slender fingers that had memories of their own.

He felt the almost forgotten heat from long ago surging upwards inside him like an urgent panic attack.

Eyes closed, bent and half crouching, the man began to play.

The ragged notes of rotten key strings and the missing slivers of ivory couldn't mask the melody of the Blue Danube waltz.

Like a dented ping pong ball in an abandoned concert hall, the sound bounced off the walls of the decaying buildings that lined the alleyway,

But nobody, nothing, could deny the magic of the music.

A fascinated dove flutters down from a nearby rooftop. Her partner landing seconds behind her. Heads cocked they absorb the sounds of the piano. He nuzzles her gently.

"Shall we?" he asks cooing along with the melody.

She nuzzles closer. Wings entwined they begin their delicate waltz. Sometimes fluttering. Sometimes skipping.

A group of gangly sunflowers cling to each other, their branches intertwined, swaying and smiling to the sounds of Strauss.

Two snails glide gracefully together in a hidden corner murmuring "slower- slower, slow-slow-slower" to one another.

A pair of synchronized dragonflies dip and dive across a tiny orange puddle created by a popsicle dropped by a pretty young girl in a pink party dress.

A woman with a walker stops at the end of the alleyway. A smile eases the wrinkles on her face as she remembers the many times she'd said 'yes' to dashing young dance partners.

A curious black tomcat pauses on its mysterious quest, a look of selfish distain on his face when he realizes that there's nothing in it for him here.

A sudden crashing reverberates throughout the alleyway, as with a violent motion the man smashes the piano lid closed and open, closed and open and closed.
The dance floor falls silent as the creatures and critters creep quietly back to their secret places.

The man looked up with eyes that were a kaleidoscope of anger, anguish, hate and helplessness. His fingers had taken him back to a time when he really thought he had a shot at making it big in the concert hall. That was before Croatia, the young girl and the explosions.
He'd never heard his wife say, 'Welcome home.'
He'd never heard her say, 'It's a girl.'
He'd never heard his daughter say, 'I love you Daddy.'
He'd never heard his daughter say, 'I do.'
He'd never heard his wife say, 'I'm leaving you.'
"God, you son of a bitch." he screamed up at dark gathering clouds. "You owe me, you bloody well owe me," his voice choking as he looked back down.

That's when he heard the thundering hail of his tears as they dripped softly onto the piano keys.

And So It Begins

The two children didn't know I was
taking this shot. I found the image and
their innocence quite captivating. To
this day, I'm curious about what were
they discussing so intensely? I obviously
had no idea so, I made it up!

.

And So It Begins

"Wanna go play hide and go seek in the cornfield?"

"My Mom says we can't go in there 'cos of the monster."

"What?"

"You can't say 'what' you have to say pardon."

"Pardon?"

"My Mom said there's a monster in there an' I can't go there."

"Scaredy cat, there's no monster, your Mom's just saying that."

"No she isn't, there is a monster in there, I've heard it."

"You're just a girl, you don't know anything about monsters."

"I'm in grade 2."

"But you're still a girl."

"My Daddy says I'm a princess."

"Yeah. in that case I'm a frog."

"Oh yuck, does that mean you have to kiss me?"

"What?"

"Pardon!"

"Pardon?"

"I said if you're a frog and I'm a princess do you have to kiss me?"

"No silly, only grown ups kiss."

"...and frogs and princesses..."

"That's just in stories and movies."

"If you kiss me does that mean we'll have babies and get married?"

"I dunno…"

"I saw this show on tv and this boy and girl were kissing and stuff and they had babies and got married."

"I saw my sister kissing her boyfriend and they didn't have babies."

"I've got a cat."

"What's it called?"

"Its name is skunk 'cos it's black with a white stripe on it's back - but my dad calls it friggin' cat."

"We've got a goldfish, it's called carrot."

"Carrot? Goldfish aren't called carrot."

"Are so. It used to be called Sam but Sam died and my Mom didn't want to tell us it died so she put a baby carrot in the goldfish bowl instead. But I know it's just a carrot, that's why I call it carrot."

"That's stupid!"

"What? I mean, pardon."

"Calling a goldfish carrot, that's stupid."

"You can't say that word, that's a bad word."

"That's silly then."

"I'll kiss you if you want?"

"You mean like rescue me from the monster?"

"Well, sure."

"Ok then…I guess."

"What's your name?"

Fish No Fish

I was struck by the cruel irony of the two signs
on this fishing hut on the east coast of
England. One boasting fish, the other, no fish.
It seemed to sum up where our world is headed
and gave birth to this poem.

Fish No Fish

Did the last fish know it was the last fish
As it floated, bloated
On the surface of a septic like sea

How will we reconcile the simple question why
With a mindless, blindness
We sentenced our seven seas to die

Did the last fish make a last wish
To let the land, withstand
our senseless slaughter, with a skeptical plea

The choice is no choice as only you and I
Can make sustainable, attainable
If with ceaseless, selfless spirit we try

It's a Spring Thing

This just tumbled out quickly while sitting on my
back deck on a glorious winter turning to spring
afternoon. The robins had just returned and the
back yard was busy! The story practically wrote
itself inspired by the goings on in my garden!

It's a Spring Thing

I saw my first robins of the year the other day. Bobbing around, bashing their beaks on the still semi frozen soil as they searched somewhat optimistically for worms.

There may be white stuff still on the ground but there's change in the air. I can smell it, feel it, almost taste it.

I find myself with an overwhelming desire to clean, to paint, to get rid of old stuff, to get in new stuff, to move things around, to change things up!

Come to think of it, this happens around this time every year. It must be a nesting thing. A Spring thing!

But back to the Robins.

I'm sure you've seen them too. Squabbling, flitting, squawking, flirting.

I've yet to figure out if the third party in the Robin's menage-a-trois is a jealous lover, the mother-in-law or the robin's Realtor doing the rounds with his prospects.

"This is a great starter tree," the Realtor might be saying, "Fabulous views, the perfect place to build, with perching room for 6 and conveniently located for worms, flying lessons and all in a blue jay free area, not that I'm prejudice of course."

There's always a lot of conversations going on between them, so

I assume that Mr & Mrs Robinson (I'll call them that to protect their true identity) are having heated discussions about the merits of their Realtor's suggested location in which to build their family nest.

Or is the 3rd party a jealous lover? I must confess that I lean towards this option. I'm convinced this third party has an Italian accent and boy oh boy, you should hear him sing! I think I'll call him Raphael. Yes, Raphael the randy Roman robin – and from the way that Mr. Robinson looks at him he looks like he'd like to a take a powerful peck at Raphael's pasta like pecker!

However, to be completely honest, the constant prattle and the beady eyes with attitude could well mean that the third party is indeed the Mother-in-Law.
I think this is actually the case as she's the one with the puffed-up breast, who never shuts up and seemingly has a bird brain opinion about everything.

They're not here today. Perhaps they're huddled together hiding from the horrendous weather.
Or maybe, they've gone their separate ways, seeking solitary refuge from the snow and sleet and communicating now only with tweets!

Either way – "Here's to you Mr. & Mrs. Robinson, Jesus loves you even when it snows."

Old Man

This wasn't an easy one to write. Now that I'm reaching a "certain age" I find that more and more I slip into times when I reflect back on my life so far. This story isn't about me though — a fictional me maybe — but it's really a potential composite of the life thoughts of all men who reach my age.

Old Man

The old man pulled a grubby handkerchief from a pocket in his pants and wiped the moisture from the stubble on his sweaty wrinkled chin.

He sighed, shuffling on the slatted metal park bench and wondered just how hot it was going to get. Almost 30 degrees he'd heard on the radio earlier. Had to be close to that now.

He felt his eye lids getting heavy, drooping. The lazy buzzing lullaby of a nearby bumble bee luring him into that no-man's land between awareness and oblivion.

There was a time he'd welcomed the warm weather and all it brought. A garden to mess around in and a wife to mess around with.

Both were gone now. He wasn't sure which he missed the most. He loved his garden. He was married to his wife.

He was still a kid when he met and married his bride, young enough to confuse love with lust. Lust turned to duty, duty became a sort of contented companionship which in turn simply came to be something that just was.

What happened to real love? He mused. *Do I miss not having really loved? Can you miss something you never had? You can yearn for it, yes but miss it?*

Had real love been denied him or had he denied real love. He didn't think he felt sorry for himself; it was more a feeling of mild puzzlement of having lived a life and not to have truly loved.

Perhaps, he rationalized, he was too preoccupied with the work of life to concern himself with the wonder of love. That what he had was a 'good enough' love, not the love of movies perhaps, but of an everyman's kind of love. Sort of. Maybe.

His thoughts meandered to the times he'd worked in his garden. Toiling, tilling, tending, nurturing each seedling until it burst into the glory of bloom, fulfilling and overwhelming him with mesmerizing, beauteous joy.

From somewhere the words *'As you sow, so shall you reap'* maneuvered through his mind.

His eyes snapped opened in faint surprise. The implications suddenly disturbingly clear. He'd not thought before of the notion and need of sowing, growing and nurturing love. Maybe if he had......

"Screw it. It's too late now anyway." he decided, closing his eyes fully and surrendering to the safety and sanctuary of sleep.

Stan Screamed

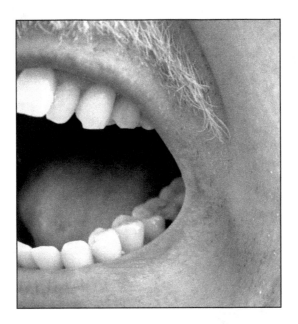

This was one of those "got to write it in 10 minutes" challenges called a prompt. There was no specific plan for this short piece. As with the writings to most prompts, some electrical surge takes place in the head and then something pops out onto the paper (or screen)!

Stan Screamed

Father Stan, bent and bowed, cassock as crinkled as his face, shuffled slowly past Finnegan's Bar on his long nightly walk home. Finnegan's and his basement apartment were both in one of the dingier areas of town.

He paused in the rain to catch his breath thinking *Father Stan, you're not getting any younger, maybe it's time to give this up and take the bus.*
A grimy taxi sped past, splattering his wet white cassock with muddy puddle water leaving the priest looking like a poor man's imitation Picasso.

He cursed a most unholy curse as he stepped back into the shelter of the awning below the 50's neon sign that flickered FINNEG N'S.
The A had been missing for some years now.

He turned to look through the steamed-up window of the bar, 'to check on the health of the heathens' as he had been heard to put it.
He froze in mid-turn, completely unable to comprehend, to accept, the sudden sight.

Stan saw. Stan shook. Stan screamed.

Gertie - A Pigs Tale

Gertie is plain selfish indulgence. An afternoon of letting my imagination overrule reality. But I hope you get to feel Gertie's pain as her quest turns out to be a bit of a bust. The photograph, by the way, has won quite a few awards. Who'd have thought? I mean, I know it's the Year of the Pig but — it is just a pig!

Gertie – A Pigs Tale

It was that time.

Moving the bucket in the corner of the stall, Gertie removed the hidden cloth left behind by the farmer's son the last time he did the mucking out.

Carefully, she covered her face snout and ears, tying the cloth tightly so it wouldn't come loose. Grabbing a pitchfork with a broken shaft she silently scuffled past her sleeping pen mates and prised open the latch to the gate that lead to the path, that lead to the world outside.

All was clear. No one was about at this early hour. She trotted down the path towards the road and her goal, just as she'd rehearsed so many times in her mind.

The sun was high when she finally saw the giant green and yellow Co-op sign. Heart pounding, she waited awhile by the side of the ribbon of black asphalt, all that lay between her and her prize. A dusty old robin's egg blue Ford truck turned into the gas pumps at the Co-op. Nothing else in sight, she crossed the black ribbon, past the pumps, pausing outside the door of the convenience store. Adjusting her mask, tightly gripping the broken pitchfork, she quietly opened the door glancing left then right, scanning the aisles.

A pimply faced teen something got up from his chair behind the counter laying down his half eaten hot dog, yellow mustard dripping from his chin.

"Your chocolate truffles," demanded Gertie gruffly. "All of them – now!" her practiced words trembling as she brandished her pitchfork in a menacing manner.

"Bbbbut you're a pig – a ppppotbellied pig," stammered the youth.

Damn thought Gertie angrily, realizing that her carefully tied mask must have slipped.

"Now!" she repeated boldly "All your chocolate truffles now!"

The pimply faced youth was struggling to think things through. His muddled early morning mind trying to remember his training. *What to do in the case of being held up by a potbellied pig* he Googled mentally. His scan didn't yield any results.

Gertie swung around abruptly and trotted past the ice cream coolers sniffing out the candy aisle.

With the pig's back turned to him the youth lunged for the phone and stabbed out 911.

Gertie made a left turn at a rack of forty three types of chewing gum and came face to face with a tempting display of Captain Crunch. She paused, thought briefly about the opportunity, but moved on.

Glancing back she saw the youth, phone in hand, staring at her. She turned to the business at hand, motivated by the scent of her objective. The chocolate truffles must be close now. A few more steps and there, just above her shoulder, box upon box of the ultimate delights.

Gertie felt an overwhelming, all pervading rush of heat pulse through her, the sound of sirens unheard. Standing on her rear legs she just managed to reach the shelf that stocked that oh-so tempting treasure for the tongue.

With a frightening crash, the metal mesh cage suddenly enveloped her, its well used bolt slamming into place sealing Gertie's fate. Frustrated and fearful she threw herself against the bars of the cage, her body writhing with rage. *so near yet so far away*, she screamed inwardly.

Tears slowly dampened her face as, from between the bars of the cage, she watched the treasure boxes of truffles slowly recede into the distance.

The two uniformed men carrying the cage that carried Gertie passed by the counter on their way to their truck parked just by the door. The pimply youth snickered and smirked through his hot dog, mustard tinged yellow face. "Hey pimple face," Gertie snorted, "I think that was my mother-in-law you just ate."

The yellow smeared face turned white.

Shadows

This photograph is meaningful to my wife and I. The two of us were walking our property a few years back and the way the sun was positioned created these fabulous shadows that stretched out in front of us. I had my camera with me (as usual) and this was the result. We went on to use this shot in our wedding invitation and it also has won a few prizes. At a much later date, it also went on to inspire the poem.

Shadows

Could shadows simply be our souls, stepping out for a brief sojourn in the sun?

Are they there to share something we should learn, or to ask us something we should know?

Are they old souls, soul mates reaching out one more time?

Do souls fall in love, make love or are they love?

Do our souls serve us, do they serve a higher entity or do we serve our souls?

Are souls different from our spirit?

Are souls what we are and spirit what we have?

Do we try to know them in the way they know and understand us?

Do we need to look outside ourselves to see inside ourselves?

Could our souls be silent shadows of our self, or could our souls be our self?

Little Star of Bethlehem

Although written as a Christmas story I think this works ongoingly. It was inspired by the memories of a visit I'd made to Bethlehem and my dealing with the many juxtapositions that exist in that town, indeed that land.

Little Star of Bethlehem

It was Zarina's 2nd week on the job and she'd already discovered that in her business, having just one leg was extremely profitable.

How else could an eight year old one legged orphan make $12 a day? Her handlers called her their 'Little Star of Bethlehem.'

The sun was bouncing off the gold leafed dome of the Church of the Nativity, just as the first of the daily brigade of buses arrived. Zarina took her place with the rest of the professional child beggars, faces greased, clothes ragged and crumpled. They all pushed and shoved for the best positions and began their wailing litany of woes; coin collecting cans held hopefully in outstretched fingers or toes as the crowds streamed by.

"Roman Catholics this way, Greek Orthodox over there and all others use the turnstile to your right," called out a guide. Fees dutifully paid, entrance was granted into the holy place where, according to legend, the one that was called Jesus Christ was born.

A wizened old woman tossed a cardboard cup to the gutter next to Zarina, the leftover smell of sweet coffee reminding her of a time when she once had a home and parents.

An overweight man dribbled some coins into her waiting can, pointed to his camera and then at her. She quickly scanned the number of coins deposited and nodded.

A lightly bearded young man on a smoke billowing motor bike slowed as he tossed a netted bag to a young woman on the Church steps and quickly drove off.
Oranges from Jaffa to sell, mused Zarina.

Up and down the street, bus after idling bus disgorged its load.
It was going to be a very profitable Christmas Eve, she thought.
And that's when the bag of oranges, the bomb and the young woman on the church steps exploded.

Lest We Forget

It was around Remembrance Day and I was putting together a montage of my photographs of old tractors that I'd taken over the years. I guess somehow I made a connection between all that November 11 represents and the pictures of the old, no longer valued tractors I was sorting through. This was a sad one to write.

Lest We Forget

There aren't so many of them now.

Their numbers diminished by time.

They gather on this day each year to remember, to give and receive tribute.

Once, these machines were the protectors and providers of our way of life. Powerful, fueled by the fervor of youth.

Leading the way forward, driven to churn up the ground, ruthlessly spitting out all in their path.

Unwavering in their duty, chopping, grinding, smashing and pulverizing, cutting down all that stood proud and defiant before them.

Maneuvering mile after mile through muck and mud, the wreckage of broken brothers abandoned around them.

Obediently, field by field, hill by hill, rut by rut, they did what needed to be done. There was no escaping their inexorable, relentless charge.

Their bodies are tired now, wearied and worn. A little stiffer, a lot slower.

But once a year, shiny in their finery, they leave the building they call home where those who were once dependent upon them now leave them tucked away, left to their memories.

With pride they parade, only to be returned home where they'll wait and wonder if they will be honoured once more.

For this day next year, there will be fewer of them again.

One Hour. One Summer.

The sight of these punt style rowing
boats conjured up a time of an
elegant, romantic, warm summer's
afternoon on the river. I wanted to
share with you how it felt to me.
Let me take you there!

One Hour. One Summer.

Hand in hand, fingers embracing, we skip with anticipation
along the rickety misshapen dock to our waiting vessel.
You, in your long flowing white dress wearing a straw hat
boasting a garland of daisies, carrying a picnic basket for me.
Me, in my white pants, black and white striped jacket and
slicked back hair, carrying a torch for you.
Admiring glances are cast our way. We smile at each other
knowing that Gatsby had nothing on us.
We stop at the hut at the end of the dock where a well weathered
sign declares that we can 'rent a piece of paradise on the river by
the hour.'
I pay and pick up a pillow for the back seat of the boat.
"Which one is ours?" you query with an excited lilt to your
voice, pointing at the waiting fleet of boats.
"Why, the best one of course," I laugh back.

I push us gently away from the dock and proudly maneuver us to
the centre of the river.
The prairie blue sky is dotted with cotton wool cumulous clouds
that smile down upon us benevolently.
An effortless breeze sends timid ripples across the water.
You settle sideways into the seat and just like a child, slide out
of your sandals, slipping your toes into the warm welcoming
water.
You sit like that for a while, at peace, pensively gazing up the
river.

I shed my shoes and join you.

The strains of a distant radio waft downstream adding, not
taking away from the moment.
Two young children argue on the shoreline, an ice cream cone
bobbing in the water in front of them. I idly wonder to myself
who's to blame?
Two dragonflies dance the diablo on their way from nowhere to
somewhere.
We glide past a weeping willow, branches touching the water,
topping up the river with its tears.
You toss your head, tussled hair sending your hat tumbling into
the river.
The garland of daisies provides a magnificent tiara for a
fortunate duck breaking through the water for a new gasp of air.

You laugh joyfully, flashing blue eyes suddenly diminishing the
river's clear azure water to a flat murky grey.
The boat dips and sways side to side as we swing our feet back
on board. You reach for the picnic basket.
Throwing open the lid, you grasp a grape and roll it playfully
across to me.
Sliding a half-eaten strawberry from between fully open lips,
you toss it towards a majestic swan that has just come begging.
A rowboat overcrowded with rowdies draws close. They jeer,
toss back their beer and noisily cruise on their way.

A rippling wave nudges the stern of the boat in their wake, in turn, nudging me closer to you.

I stand, take a tentative step towards you, the boat left to bob and drift left to right.

You stand, looking directly at me, eye to eye.

Another step. Our toes touch.

You stay standing, unmoving, eyes still locked on mine. Calm. Waiting.

I reach out, my arms inviting you.

You lean forward, accepting my invitation.

Perspiration films on your upper lip.

Your hand reaches for my cheek, your forefinger tracing an arc from my nose to just beneath the dimple in my chin.

You leave it there. I feel it trembling. Your finger beckons me, the motion moving my face to yours.

My mind explodes with impossible possibilities.

My body a melting snowman surrendering to the heat of your intense gaze.

I jerk back from the threshold, a tumultuous tsunami of emotions swamping me.

I whisper hoarsely those three simple, complicated, life changing words.

"I am married!"

It Seems To Me

This is a story that started out as being an attempt to write works using each of the teachings of the Ten Commandments in a modern day setting. This version of "Thou shalt not kill" didn't want to go much further than it did. So now, it's a short story.

It Seems to Me

"You're a damned fool," Dave's mother spat out when he told her he was going up to the Yukon to shack up with Veronica. "You're a fool messin' with that tramp. You sure as hell must want badly what's between the legs of that pocked marked camel looking whore because it sure can't be what's between her ears."

"But Ma..."

"Don't but Ma me, seems to me your Father was a fool and you're a fool too. Seems to me the apple don't fall far from the tree."

"Now you leave Pa out of this, you went and drove him away with your naggin' just the way you're naggin' me now."

"Naggin'…NAGGIN?" Seems to me I'm the only one in this house who ever had any sense. And wipe that look off you face. You look like a pig who don't know where to poke, 'cept of course you think you do, and that pigs name is Veronica. Seems to me…."

"Shut up, you just shut up, you hear me!" Dave cut across her rant kicking the cat's dish across the kitchen floor to punctuate his point.

"You little snot bastard," Ma snarled. "Where the hell do you get off talkin' to me like that. Seems to me if you were a younger again I'd wash your mouth out with salt and…"

"Yeah, but I'm not a kid anymore am I? Anyways, I'm headed up North and you sure as hell can't stop me."

His Mother reached up and slapped him hard in the face. Left side first. Then right. Her jagged finger nails leaving a red road map on his skin.

"You stupid little piece of shit. Seems to me you think you know it all without even livin' any life."

"If your Father were here right now, don't matter how big you are, he'd take a belt to you without so much as a conversation."

Dabbing with a dirty finger at the blood beginning to ooze on his cheek Dave thought back on his Father. *No way that would happen. After all those years with Ma the poor bastard had nothing left. At least he'd dug deep and somehow found the balls to get outta here. Just like he was gonna do right now.*

Ma's old ginger-tomcat came over to mince around, weaving in and out of his worn boots, rubbin' its scrawny, fight-scarred body against his legs.

He hated that cat. Blackie, Ma called him. Dunno why, it seemed pretty stupid to him. One of Ma's rare stabs at trying to be funny he guessed.

Ma was still rambling and ranting. She wasn't much on mincin' words. The damned cat was still mincin' around him though.

Screw this. I've had enough, thought Dave.

He reached down and snatched the meat knife off the greasy kitchen table and grabbed the beat up Blackie by its tail. Both the cat and Ma began squawking like scared shitless seagulls.

Holding up the cat in front of Ma's crumpled face he swept the knife down, perfectly parting the cat's tail from its ass.

The ginger creature and Ma were howling in harmony now as cat-blood burst from Blackie's backside and the rest of the cat met the kitchen floor with a thud.

Dave had a knife in one hand, the cat's tail in the other and a decision to make.

He threw the knife back down on the table, grabbed a fist full of Ma's hair, jerked back her head and thrust the cat's tail deep into her wide open screaming mouth shoving it all the way down her throat.

He twisted the blood-soaked tail harder to stuff it all the way down. Ma twisted and wrestled with it to force it back up.

She was gagging and sagging to the floor now, struggling like a half dead raccoon in a green garbage bag. He let her fall, her eyes protruding like those on an old potato.

Dave kicked what was left of the cat which went skidding across the dirty vinyl floor till it collided with the plywood cupboards under the sink. Blackie's blood painting red graffiti art on the white doors.

Silently he turned and walked through the blood and the puke to the back door and Veronica. He gave his Ma's lifeless body a loving kick on the way past.

"Well Pa," he spoke aloud, "I guess I just did what you always wished you had. Seems to me."

I Know Her

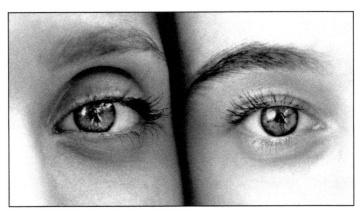

You've probably been there. That déjà-vu moment
when you think you know someone but it's perhaps,
not quite right. An alternative version of who you
remember. It happened to me recently. This short
piece is the result of that experience.

I Know Her

I knew her
We had shared each other
We had loved each other
I knew her

We laughed at our secret and unique jokes
We scorned those wiser than our years
We threw popcorn down the shorts of others
We thumbed our noses at the world

I may get to know this one
We may share one another
We may love one another
I may get to know her

I have a sense, a fear of the known
I have been here before, I know her
This is different but the same
Shit. Is this our daughter?

A Pet Peeve About Priorities

There were two items, back to back on the
news. The first was about a woman who had
written a $50,000 cheque for an animal
shelter. The second dealt with the plight of a
million plus starving children in an African
country. I know we can't fix everything but
to me it just seemed kind of mixed up. That's
when I wrote this.

A Pet Peeve about Priorities

A child cries and dies. Bloated stomach full of nothing.

A champagne flute overflows at a fundraiser harvesting money
to spoil unwanted pets
Their conscience appeased, guests provide a good living for
smart entrepreneurial vets
A woman writes a cheque for a vulgar amount to help cats live
high off the hog
A million hungry orphans barely exist in conditions not fit for a
dog

A woman is bludgeoned and battered and seeks refuge in an
underfunded shelter
A life turned topsy turvey, in an upside down world of mixed up
confused helter skelter
A child reels from blows thrown by a drunken father, the event a
quiet secret, something to hide
A dog is beaten, headlines scream, a community, sensitivities
shocked, opens it's wallets wide

A hungry frightened child shares a cardboard home with equally impoverished rats

A philanthropic businessman forms a foundation to fund a fortune for dogs and for cats

A child is killed by a bomb, thrown by a man with an immoral, illogical hate

A man kills a police dog, laws with jail time pass swiftly, to deter acts with a similar fate

Another child cries and dies. Bloated stomach full of nothing.

The Meaning of Love - A Quest

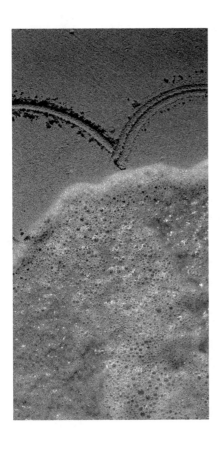

Written for, and presented at, a Valentines Day gathering, this is a semi-humorous romp with our 'hero" found dashing around Hawaii searching for the true meaning of love. He finds himself in a variety of situations which in the end, only confuse and confound his quest. But, of course, there has to be a happy ending. Or does there?

The Meaning of Love – A Quest

I got an e-mail newsletter the other day from one of those internet marketing gurus. It was signed 'with much love' Holly. I've never met Holly and, frankly, didn't realize that we were that close!

And then, at brunch the other week I was told 'I love your socks', how much our friends 'loved seafood' and that they just 'loved our new car.'

That's a whole lot of loving and it got me to wondering what the heck is love anyway?

That's when the idea to search for, and perhaps discover, the true meaning of love began to percolate. Yes, I would embark on a quest!

"Why Hawaii?" asked my wife, somewhat dubiously when I announced my plans, "And why alone?"

"Everyone says that Hawaii is the island of love and who ever heard of a man taking his wife on a quest. Sir Lancelot sure didn't, and it's just for a couple of days anyway."

I'll skip her comebacks about my being sexist and won't bother with the details of the long night I spent on the couch. Alone.

It was Tuesday morning and the Rockies were eight kilometres below. The Beatles were singing All You Need Is Love in my ears as the flight attendant stopped right next to my seat with her trolley. I took out my earphones, asked for an apple juice, checked out her name tag and started my research.

"Hey Melanie" I said, "I'm on a quest to find out the meaning of love. Do you mind if I ask what loves means to you?"

She gave me my juice together with a very suspicious look.

"You're not a lawyer are you?" she asked abruptly, "Did my husband put you up to this?"

I answered no to both questions. She looked nervously around the cabin, leaned forward and whispered into my ear.

"I'll tell you what love is," she hissed, "love is having to spend hour after hour in this damned aluminum tube being a glorified economy class geisha girl because I've got two kids I love at home that I have to feed, clothe, provide them with dance lessons, basketball camp and then put away money for their education, pay the rent, pay the bills and I've got an always-out-of-work, lazy, useless son of bitch of a husband who's a no good for nothing lush. So you've gotta do what you gotta do to make life work. Does that answer your question?"

I gulped and nodded. Melanie stood up and with a bright professional smile insisted that I enjoy my flight! I put my headphones back on just as Elvis was singing Love Me Tender.

So, love is unthinking, it's caring, it means responsibility, love is totally unselfish. Is love the opposite of hate, or, do we hate love and love hate?

After landing, I picked up a porter who picked up my bag at the whirling crowded carousel and walked towards the exit to grab a cab.

"Aloha…welcome to Hawaii," said the girl straight out of an award winning travel brochure.

My heart beat faster, "Aloha to you too," I smiled my most charming smile as she placed a lei around my neck.

"I'm in Hawaii to find out about love," I said, my smile now working overtime.

She looked at me with a coy, sweet, appraising gaze. "Huana koola kali wapa sudo ki papa" she answered, her face telling me in no uncertain terms that not only had I come to the right place, but that I was also a good candidate to find love.

She walked away glancing back at me as she left. "What was it she said?" I asked my porter eagerly.

"Girl said get out of her face you dirty old man." "Hmm" I murmured and made a mental note, *Love can be misunderstood and can it be two faced sometimes?*

I had a sip of my morning coffee looking down from my balcony on an already crowded Waikiki Beach. As I picked up the morning newspaper strains of the old song, Love is a Many Splendor Thing drifted up from the beach.

Wait a minute! There it was, right on page four. The adv. screamed boldly 'Are You Looking For Love?' I grabbed the phone with mounting anticipation, stabbed out the number in the adv. and a girl answered in a sing-song voice.

"Good morning, are you looking for love?"

"Yes, yes, I am" I answered "I'm here in Hawaii looking for the meaning of love."

"How much love you want?" she asked, "you want fifteen minute love, thirty minute love or the sixty minute all you can enjoy love?"

"No, no," I mumbled into the phone realizing the mistake I'd made, a big mistake. "I'm looking for the kind of love that might last a lifetime."

"Hey Mister, our girls good but no can do a lifetime of love. You don't want love, you want a relationship."

I hung up sweating, thinking *how wrong could I have been? Is love lust. Can you have love without lust or lust without love? What's the difference between love and a relationship? What is a relationship any way* …but wait, that's a separate quest!"

As I left the hotel a couple walked towards me holding hands, they were maybe in their late sixties, him wearing a Hawaiian shirt and her wearing a matching mumu.

Ah-haa, these two look as though they know the meaning of love.

I stepped forward. "Excuse me but you two look so happy together I was wondering if you had found true love?"

"You bet," said mumu woman "Were celebrating our fortieth anniversary on this trip."Her husband smiled at her proudly.

"We're from Cleveland, Ohio," she continued as if that explained everything.

"Forty years" I said, "Well congratulations, you two must truly understand the meaning of love?"

The husband gave me a puzzled look. "Love?" he queried, "You mean like in the movies?"

"Well sort of" I said, "Sometimes, in some movies I guess."

They looked at each other with blank stares, "Well, I don't know about that," said mumu woman, "but we are best friends, we're used to each other if you know what I mean?"

"We're content, we know each other and what we like," added her husband."

"But what about the bells and whistles – what about gut churning feelings for each other?"

The man began to turn red, shuffling his feet in an agitated way. "Now listen fella, why don't you just move along…."

"Yes," added mumu woman, "Don't you go spoiling our anniversary with your dumb questions."

I left them looking at each other with scared expressions and doubt on their faces.

I continued on my way, thinking about the couple from Cleveland, wondering, *Is love measured in years? Is it based on time together? Could love just be a comfortable habit?*

BANG – preoccupied with the couple from Ohio, I walked right into a sign board sitting on the sidewalk outside of a gleaming new condo tower. 'Adonis Towers – You're Going to Love It Here' screamed the bright red sign.

Hmmmm – got to check this out, I thought.

I followed a long red carpet, flanked on both sides by dozens of grass skirt clad girls and bronzed half naked young men, all hypnotically swaying, their waving palm fonds keeping time with the romantic sounds of a Hawaiian guitar. The music stopped and the entourage sank to their knees as a women in a glittering gold gown swept in and seated herself upon the throne. "Welcome to Adonis Towers, I am the goddess of real estate, the one who will make all your dreams of love come true," she announced.

"I saw your sign," I mumbled suitably humbled, "And wanted to ask you about the meaning of love."

"Love?" thundered the goddess, "Love? Love is living here at Adonis Towers. You're gonna love it here. Life at Adonis Towers means you'll love yourself, you'll love the way you live with no responsibilities. Your friends will envy your hedonistic way of life. Be as selfish as you want to be. For you, I would recommend our Narcissus Suite, wall to wall mirrors in every room for just $90,000 down and $2800 a month – on approved credit of course!"

I stumbled back out on to the street, caught my breath and paused thinking, *Is love really selfish or is it unselfish? Can you love others without loving yourself? Is loving yourself more important than loving others?*

I headed down to the beach to walk awhile to clear my head.

"I'm sorry." I said to the surfer dude as I accidentally kicked sand all over his board. An Adonis himself, he was wearing a yellow T-shirt emblazoned with the purple words Love Is A 20ft Wave on the front. "Hey man, no sweat, remember love means never having to say you're sorry."

"Aaah, but love is also a 20ft wave." I replied cleverly, reading off his T-shirt.

"Too true man, love is a 20ft wave on the board. You find it, ride it as long as you can, then it wipes out. You come off the high, pick yourself up and go hunting for the next wave."

My surfer dude took off, running into the ocean with his board. I assumed he was looking for his next wave, his next love.

I sat on the silky soft sand and played back our conversation. *So love isn't necessarily a one-time thing, but can real love be found again and again?*

I yawned, my head nodded and I drifted, thoughts of love meandering through my mind. Then, giving myself up to the warmth of the sun, I slipped into sleep.

I began to dream a of a beautiful woman in a long flowing white dress boasting a garland of bougainvillea's in her hair. Together we floated on the waves, laughing, playing under a sinful sun. Time had no meaning for us and I felt a love, what I call love, that I'd never felt before.

I woke up groggy and wet, my dream shattered, as waves of water swept over my legs and waves of guilt swept over me. Just a dream I reassured myself. It was just a dream. But in my memory lingered a vision of the beautiful woman in the long flowing white dress with bougainvillea's in her hair.

Back at the hotel bar, thinking about my dream, I thought, *Is infatuation the precursor to love, or, is it a form of love itself. Is infatuation to love - as fad is to fashion?*

The rainbow colours of a gay pride flag hung above the bottles at the back of the not so busy bar.

A young man with the most beautiful hair I think I'd ever seen along with a girl about the same age, who's head was fully shaven, were busy not working.

"What can I get you?" said the girl.

"A beer and the answer to a question." I replied, sounding like Bogart at his best.

"The beer is easy, what's the question?" asked my bald-headed Bacall.

"What is love?" I asked.

"Hey Mike," called the girl to the young man with the hair, "this guy wants to know what love is."

"Don't we all?" Mike replied, putting down a handful of clean glasses and turning towards me. "What is love?" he repeated wistfully.

"Well to me love is a bit like a trip to the casino, sometimes you win, sometimes you lose. You sit in on the game, you draw a straight or handful of queens. You can't choose the cards you're dealt. So like everyone else in the game you play them the best way you can."

"Some follow suit, some bluff, some hold their cards close to their chest, some don't want to play the game so they fold. "You can't choose the cards you're dealt, you can only choose how to play them."

"Yes," I interrupted, "but that's life – not love."

"But isn't love like life though?" the bald-headed girl chimed in, "I mean isn't love just a manifestation of the choices you make in life?"

I paid my bill and left for my room thinking, *Is love really like life, do you choose who and how you love or is it preordained?* I pondered this for a while.

Boarding my homebound plane I had just buckled up my seat belt when a weary but cheery voice cried "Hey, it's you!"

"Hey Melanie."

"What's with you, how did it go, your quest? Did you figure out the meaning of love?"

She slammed the overhead bin shut with a loud bang, precisely punctuating the word love.

"I think I'm more confused than when I started." I replied, looking up at her. "My quest seemed to turn up more questions than answers."

"What do you mean?" She asked with her eyebrows.

"Well, for example….is love caring – is it compassionate?

Is love work or a joy?

Is love selfish or unselfish or both?

Is it about friendship?

Can it be simply a habit?

Can love be a fleeting interlude or does it last a lifetime?

Are love and lust mistaken for each other?

Can love be misunderstood or a missed opportunity?

Is love transparent? Or is it two-faced?

Is love by choice or by chance?

Is it random or preordained?

Is love real or is it imagined?"

Melanie moved on looking preoccupied with my revelations about love, deep in her own thoughts… leaving me to mine.

Eleven hours later I opened my front door. I smelled the familiar vanilla candles. Bing Crosby was crooning the old song True Love in the background.

"Aloha" I called out, "I'm home."

Your Choice of Endings Follow

The Happy Ending:

"Aloha to you to," replied my wife from the living room. I walked through. She got up from the couch to greet me.

"Before you say anything to me, I've got something I want, I need, to say to you." I blurted out.

She looked at me questioningly.

"I don't know why I feel the way I do but...I love you."

It was quiet for a moment. Then she smiled at me, "I know." she replied simply, standing there looking like a dream come true in a long white dress wearing a welcome tiara of bougainvillea's in her hair.

The Not So Happy Ending:

"Oh crap." I heard my wife cursing from the living room. I walked through. She got up from the couch covering her naked top with a cushion to greet me.

"You're back home sooner than I thought. But before you say anything to me I've got something I want, I need, to say to you," she blurted out."

I looked at her questioningly.

"This has never happened before, it's just that when you said..."

"Get outtta here." I said to Ricky, who until now was my best friend.

Taught Boy Learning

This is another incredibly powerful
photograph by Carolyn Haggart. The
sadness, sullenness and secret fears
oozing out of this young mans face was
me many years ago when, just a
youngster, I lost my mother. This one
was tough to write and, even now,
tough to read.

Taut Boy Learning

Piss off you inconsequential old bag
Time is a great healer you say
What do you know you nosey old hag
It's not your Mother just taken away.

What unkind god makes these kinds of choices
Answer that you stupid old cow
'Time's a great healer' chime in other voices
Tell me all of you, just what happens now?

It's not your fault you're the bore from next door
You're just taking the brunt of my grief
It's your almighty god I hate and abhor
So much for blind faith and belief.

You're just trying to be a good neighbour
And part of me does understand
You too were shocked by her departure
One that only your god guy had planned.

Please don't cry, be remorseful or sad
Time is a great healer they say
It's not you that's making me mad
But god playing in his own selfish way.

She Knows the Way

I must confess to this being a favourite of mine. It was inspired by my friend Barbara who is one of those individuals that seems to connect with that other space, that zone that is just beyond most of us. She is a poet and perhaps even a prophet and, somehow, she knows the way of things!

She Knows the Way

She Knows the Way of Life

She knows the secrets shared by dry rattling bones as they
whisper hidden truths to each other.

Why ravens in black, cackle quietly before swooping, to swarm
and mourn a dead mother.

She knows why lesser creatures destroy delicate structures spun
by workaholic spiders.

Why dragonflies whirl and twirl, as they change their minds en-
route from nowhere to somewhere.

She Knows the Way of Dreams

She knows why a fine vintage red pours from a hole in her heart
and flows into a bottomless glass.

Why a black and white cat plays a piano piece from Poland
while driving a Korean Sonata.

She knows why strange women, serenade her seductively,
showing off their penetrating vibratos.

Why a pontificating priest dressed up like a dentist can pull
telling truths from her mouth.

She Knows the Way of Love

She knows the sweet delicious guilt, the rewarding delight, of stealing another wife's life.

Why an old flame fires then fades during an indulgent reunion, mere embers of a younger encounter.

She knows that saying I love you can be caring, or careless, each bringing pain in a singular way.

Why sons turn into daughters and mothers become fathers and a man takes fourteen more wives.

She has the sight. She sees the truths.

She knows the way of things.

Just Another Old Man

I was waiting for a friend outside the front of a local retirement residence on a gorgeous sunny morning when out wheeled an elderly gentleman who made his way to the smoking area. He lit a cigarette and just stared into space. I wondered what he could have been thinking. This story is what may have been going through his mind.

Just Another Old Man

Old Jake's arthritic hands painfully maneuvered his wheelchair through the automatic doors leading out of the seniors' home.
The doors slid closed behind him with a splutter, a hiss and a deafening clunk.
Jake had always figured that was what prison doors sounded like.
Ten times a day he made the pilgrimage from the confines of his quarters to his mecca that was the smoking area - just by the green lawn that lay between the front doors and the parking lot.
He had it timed.
Eight minutes there and eleven minutes back.
There was no good reason to rush back.

Under the warm sun, his cold body squirmed in his wheelchair.
His gnarled nicotine stained fingers fumbled in his pants pocket searching for another hit for his habit.
He stopped moving, feeling a warmth blanketing his groin.
He looked down watching the wet stain spreading slowly across his crumpled grey polyester pants.
It looks a bit like Africa, a dark grey map of Africa, he thought idly.
Ashamed, he pulled the damp pack from his pocket, selected a smoke and placed it to his quivering lips.
Frustrated, two trembling hands clasped and finally clicked the lighter. He inhaled his reward.

'Frustration is fuel for finding a new way that suits you better,' someone once said to him. He had always remembered that for some reason.

But what suits me better is not to be the new me. I want the old me. But come to think about it I am the old me, the new old me.

A perky robin hopped past a nearby 'Please stay off the grass sign' pecking at the ground, on a mission maybe to find food for its family.

A fancy new silver SUV swept into the driveway. *Old Agnes Carrigan's daughter making her twice weekly visit to see her Mom,* he thought.

Funny to think of a grandmother Agnes's age being someone's daughter.

Daughters are young women aren't they?

Wonder whether she comes out of caring or guilt?

He thought about his own kids. Only the two girls left now. The two boys gone.

He eyes leaked. *A man isn't supposed to live longer than his children,* he thought.

Come to think of it, the girls haven't been here for a while.

 "Sorry Dad, I'm just busy busy busy." their mantra rang in his ears.

He remembered back to when he was so busy. Everything seemed so important at the time.

The familiar feeling of guilt teeter tottered at the edge of his consciousness, and his conscience.

Had he been a good father?

Could I have done better. God knows I tried, but maybe it was too little too late.

I wonder if there is a God? Well, I'll find out soon enough, he mused.

I guess Ed found out, thinking about his smoking buddy who took his final drag last week.

The chip chirp chip of the robin caught his attention again. There were two of them now, pecking together. *Mr & Mrs,* he assumed, *sharing the family chores, working as a team to feed the kids. Bring them up right. Don't go there,* he thought, shuffling uncomfortably in his wheelchair.

Jake realized that he got to this point everyday nowadays. The point when he'd think about Mabel his wife. She'd been gone for a while now. Thought about what was, about what could have been.

The sound of a car cut through his reverie.

An older lady, they were all mostly older ladies now it seemed, stepped carefully out of a green Ford van that drew up outside the doors. He recognized the same pink jacket that she always wore when she came. Every day at 3.30. Right on the dot.

Marie, he recalled her name.

He remembered because the first time he'd met her she'd introduced herself by giving him a Sweet Marie candy bar.

"You'll not forget sweet Marie," she chuckled.

Marie dabbled at being eighty something.

She was a volunteer who in her words "Helped drive the old folks where ever they wanted to go." A narrow smile formed small dimples on his stubbled chin. *Eighty something and she calls them old folks.*

A young looking nurse came out through the doors, passing sweet Marie on her way in.
Very nice, thought Jake, suddenly as perky as his robin friend, **very** *nice.*
He imagined her without the short skirt and her skimpy white blouse. He considered their togetherness, the soft moans, the hard response.
Deep in dark grey Africa a volcano threatened to erupt.
He held the vision for a moment then let it go. His smile retreating as slowly as the rumbling volcano.

He just sat there silently and sighed. Sadly understanding that what was, will never be again.
The sadness slipped sideways surrendering to thinking about just whatever time was left.
He thought about that a lot, spending whatever time was left thinking about whatever time was left.
He was saved from himself by the sound of a siren coming from the roadway, getting louder and louder as it got closer, blue lights flashing as it came to a stop just yards from the doors to the jail.
It wasn't really a jail of course, he just thought of it that way.

He'd once heard one of the staff call the residents inmates.
She wasn't wrong. They were all prisoners back in there.
Sentenced for life either by circumstances, or by their families,
just for committing the ultimate crime of being old.
Or of being seen to be old, he corrected himself.
Yes, they see an old shell. But no, they don't see me.
His cigarette, burned down now, dropped to the driveway.
He just stared at it and stared at it, eyes closing.

———

As I feel my eyes closing, I feel a gentle tissue harshly wiping
unknown spittle from my chin. I look up. The indifferent eyes of
she who looks after me meet mine.
"Time for your medication Jake," she shares loudly with the
world.
Why does she shout? I'm not deaf.
"Had another little itsy-bitsy accident, did we?" she announces
in her kindergarden teacher's sing-song voice.
Why does she talk to me as if I was a child?
I hate that voice.
I hate that woman.
I hate all this.
I look down as my shame wells up, starting in my gut and
spilling over into my eyes.
I wonder…
Why does dignity have to die before I do?

Sisters

I couldn't resist taking this photograph. It was so, well, so perfect. The ladies had no idea I was taking it. To me, this had to be two sisters having a conversation. However, like so many conversations it was probably pretty banal, so that's what I wrote, but I couldn't resist a bit of a zinger at the end to cut through the mundane meanderings.

Sisters

"I think that tree's got some kind of fungus."

"What do you mean fungus?"

"Well it's got knobby splotches all over its branches."

"Hmmm. They should do something about that."

"Did you hear that Edith Wilkinson died?"

"That's a shame."

"Well she was a hundred and two, died in her sleep she did."

"It's still a shame but they'll have a nice funeral for her they will. Did I tell you I had to get a tooth done?"

"Does it hurt?"

"Not now… they fixed it didn't they!"

"Well that couldn't have been cheap."

"Cost me a fortune it did, they shouldn't be allowed to get away with it."

"I know, I know. I told you old Vera Wilson had new windows put in, didn't I?"

"What does she want with new windows at her age?"

"Myrna Chadwick said it was her son-in-laws idea, keep up what the house is worth for when she's gone."

"Greedy bugger, they shouldn't allow it."

"Not too windy today is it?"

"Cloudy though, they said it might rain. I bought some fish last night for me and my Harry. I got it home and it turned out it was from China."

"China! That's awful isn't it."

"They should do something, they should."

"Going to bingo later are you?"

"Rita won $320 at bingo last week and she's as deaf as a doorpost."

"I know, I was there."

"They shouldn't allow it, should they? I mean if you can't even hear the numbers properly then how can you...

"**Mabel!** Do you think our Mom loved you more than she loved me?"

"I think you're right about that tree – they should do something they should."

Who Cares!

Gene runs the wonderful Café Verve here in Medicine Hat. He can also churn out some pretty mean bass guitar runs as well. Each month Café Verve hosts an Open Mic for writers and musicians and in conversations one day we decided to team up for the next Open Mic. Gene would play his bass guitar to my spoken writing piece. So if 'Who Cares' sounds a little like a blues song here and there, you now know why. And yes, it was a blast!

Who Cares!

I was strolling down the path of life one day
Thinking about a whole bunch of stuff on the way
Nuisance stuff, pain in the ass stuff
The stuff that smug looking people don't have to worry about
Smug bastards.
Then I figured out just why they looked so smug
They had life figured out
And I hadn't…to tell the truth my life was a bit of a drag
Because….
I was carrying around a hundred pounds of crap in a one pound
bag.

People say that they know themselves
Who they are
What they want to see
That they know about life
With its love, hate and - indifference
Living all they think they can be.

Achieving
Believing
Conforming
Performing

A society of well behaved clowns.

Say WHAT, I say,
Say WHAT?

I'm still trying to think it all through
Who I am
And what I believe
What this life's all about
Full of questions and doubt
Is that real or just what I perceive?

Some teachers and preachers they said
Hey listen
Man, you just gotta believe
Buy into what we say
And we'll show you the way
Guess they thought I was pretty naïve.

Say WHAT, I say,
Say WHAT?

What stories they told, what visions they sold
Just stuff, smoke and mirrors stuff.
They didn't care about me
And they're all pretty rich

Rich bastards
Then I figured out why they didn't really care
It was 'cos they didn't really care!

Say WHAT, I say,
Say WHAT?

Caring isn't a technique or a ploy
It's who we are
What we should embody
You just gotta let it come in
And let that feeling begin
That turns a someone into a somebody.

It's about taking the time out
It's that simple
It's not about how long life lasts
It's all to do with how it's lived
And caring is tomorrows selfless gift
Making up for lost time in the past.

Transforming
Rewarding
Satisfying
Gratifying
Helping others feel good about themselves.

I guess I knew all along, just what this was about

But had to look way inside to let it all out

So, I rearranged my priorities

Figured out what really counts

Now I walk around looking smug

Smug bastard me

And life's no longer a drag

Because....

Now I'm carrying around one hundred pounds of caring in a one pound bag!

What's in a Name?

This is a Christmas story that has meaning at anytime of the year. And it has nothing to do with the birth of Christ. 'What's in a Name' has probably provoked more reaction from readers than almost anything else I've written, both positive and negative. Now it's your turn, so you be the judge!

What's in a Name?

There were just the three of them in his private chamber.

The others were waiting next door in the Great Ice Hall.

"So, it's like this," Rudolph said, shuffling his hooves as he focused intensely on the tinsel star just above Santa's head.

"It's like what?" replied Santa, tapping his fingers on the arms of his throne, "C'mon man, spit it out."

"Yes, well, that's the point."

"What is the point?", fingers drumming faster.

"The man part."

Santa just sighed.

"I umm, I…well, I'd like to be called Rhonda."

"Rhonda." said Santa flatly, fingers suddenly still.

"Umm, yes, Rhonda."

Rudolph silently, slowly counted the points on the tinsel star.

"one… two… three… four… five."

Silence.

Rudolph counted again.

"one… two… three… four… five."

Still no response.

"one… two… three…"

The silence was suddenly shattered by Donner snickering.

"Rhonda?" repeated Santa.

Rudolph took a deep breath, tore his gaze away from the tinsel star and looked Santa straight in the eyes.

"Yes. Rhonda!" he said.

"And you?" said Santa warily to Donner, really not wanting to deal with this, "I guess you want to be called Delores or something?"

"Oh no. No…no…no. Not me. I'm good. I'm Donner through and through. Yep, that's me, Donner. Donner, I'm that. Yep, all the way. That's me. No Delores for me. I'm just…."

"Yeah yeah, OK." interrupted Santa.

"…here to support him, umm her, er, they."

He turned back to Rudolph. "So tell me son…

"No, not son, daughter maybe but I'm not quite…"

"Whatever…how did… where did…I mean what's going on here?"

"Well, I've never really felt, like, 100% right being a guy reindeer ever since I knew anything about being a guy reindeer." blurted out Rudolph, "Then about a year ago I decided to change my diet. I started grazing on special herbs and leaves, working out differently, my antlers began to shrink a bit. …it all just seemed the right thing to do. Things began to change. It was how I saw things. My attitude toward others and situations. I felt different. The way I think I was meant to be."

His voice shaking, Rudolph took another deep breath. "And then…and then something awful, wonderful…I mean scary and incredible happened. And I just couldn't hide the new me anymore. What am I saying?... I didn't want to hide the new me anymore!"

Santa leaned forward, his hand gently stroking Rudolph's ear, reassuring him, calming him down. "Tell me what happened," he spoke gently.

"My nose…my nose…it was turning pink."

There was a snicker again from Donner which was promptly cut short by a withering look from Santa.

"Carry on," said Santa.

"I thought that would be the end. I mean to all the kids in the world, to you, to all the other reindeer, to everyone, I'm supposed to be Rudolph the Red Nosed Reindeer. Not the one with the pink nose! But I want to be, have to be, Rhonda the Pink Nose Reindeer. I feel really good about myself for the first time in my life. You know, the way I was supposed to be. The real me."

Rudolph waited.

Donner waited.

"You've talked about this with the others, have you?"

"They all know," said Rudolph, "Most of them are supportive of me wanting to be the real me."

"So where do we go from here?" asked Santa. "What do you want from me?"

"To be honest, I hadn't really thought that through too much, my big thing was to get it off my chest. To hope that you would understand. Even to accept me as a pink nosed reindeer. I couldn't even focus on preparing the routes for this year's deliveries."

Santa nodded. "Well, I've got to tell you it's a bit of a shock although, I must say that I had noticed your nose seemed much paler. I respect your decision of course and as you know, we acknowledge and respect diversity here at the North Pole. Heck, we've got several thousand vertically challenged workers!" Rudolph chuckled, thinking of all Santa's elves.

"Every year on my travels around the world I see great changes in our societies. And along with those changes, more openness, greater understanding, acceptance and tolerance."

Santa leaned forward, "I think the world could be ready to accept a pink nosed reindeer. Anyway, I'm just philosophizing now, so enough of that." said Santa, "Let's go and join the others, I'm sure they're all waiting to find out what happened in here."

Rudolph, Santa and Donner walked through into the Great Ice Hall where the rest of Santa's reindeers were gathered. Muted conversations stopped as the three of them entered.

"Rudolph and I have spoken," announced Santa, "And from this moment forward he, or rather, they, will be known as Rhonda - Rhonda the Pink Nosed Reindeer. What say all of you? All in favour say aye."

There was an excited chorus of cheers. Rhonda's pink nose perked up with pride. "Aye" they shouted one after another, "Aye" they cried. All of Santa's reindeer, that was, except one.

"I can't…I just can't." spoke Vixen shaking his head.

The Great Ice Hall fell silent. Seven sets of antlers swung towards Vixen.

"Oh crap," thought Santa, "Here we go, I should have known." Only Mrs. Claus knew that Vixen was Santa's least favourite reindeer.

"It's abhorrent. It's not right." said Vixen, "We were made in His image. This is wrong! Firstly, it's not natural, secondly the world knows Rudolph as Rudolph with a red nose, not pink, and thirdly…and thirdly, well, it's just not right!"

Nobody spoke. Rhonda walked slowly over to Vixen and gently nuzzled him with her antlers.

"There is no wrong Vixen. There is no right. We can all be the same. We can all be different. We don't need to be categorized, do we? Can't we just be? We are who we are. What we are. What we choose to be, what we are chosen to be."

"I feel blessed because I have been chosen to be what I am. And I have chosen to accept this. Equally, you are blessed to be who and what you are. I'm still me Vixen, just a different version of me. And my new version loves you as much as the old version, don't you see?"

"I wanna be known as Danielle," shouted Dasher breaking the tension in the Hall.

"Put me down for Justin," said Dancer.

"Justin?" laughed Comet.

"Oh, OK then, how about Deborah."

"And I'll take Priscilla," Prancer jumped in.

"I like the sound of Claire," cried Comet.

"And I just love the sound of Caroline," said Cupid.

"And I'll be Donna," Donner threw in.

"But you're already Donna," said Dasher.

They all laughed except Vixen.

"No, not Donner like Donner, I mean Donna! Donna with an A."

"Put me down for Brittany," said Blitzen.

"Hey Vixen," called out Prancer, "What about you, what do you want to be called."

The Great Ice Hall fell silent.

Vixen scowled but said "OK, I'll play your game if I have to. I guess I could be Vivian."

As the team started singing Rhonda the Pink Nosed Reindeer, Rhonda turned back to Vixen smiling, "Vixen," she said, "I really want to thank you for..."

"Shut up you little perverted, pink nosed piece of pig shit." hissed Vixen. "Just make sure you stay at the front of the rig. Stay way away from me you hear? I don't want to be riding anywhere near some transgender weirdo, you got it?"

Reeling back, Rhonda's eyes opened wide.

She dipped her head as she turned away.

A solitary tear trickled down towards her nose.

As it touched…that pink glowing beacon of pride and hope, faded to black.

The Promise

I guess to a certain extent this is the ultimate love story, one based on complete trust. It's short and simple and, I think, somewhat sweet. Thinking about it now, I believe this was triggered by an item I heard on the news.

The Promise

"You promise you'll meet me there?"

"I promise."

"We've waited so very long for this."

She just smiled.

"I've just got to get some things out the way and I'll be there."

"It's going to be wonderful isn't it, to be together finally?"

She just smiled.

"But you will be there, you promise?"

"I promise."

"We'll do all the things that we were never able to do here."

"We won't have to pretend any more will we?"

She just smiled.

"You promise you'll be waiting?"

"I promise."

"We'll be free won't we, free from all responsibilities."

"You go now and we'll be together soon enough."

She just smiled.

"We will won't we, you promise?"

"I promise."

She slipped away silently, shimmering as she left the room.
He sifted and shuffled through the letters he'd leave, organizing
them quite precisely.

He poured his pink pills into the toilet bowl and flushed.

He looked around, nodded his satisfaction and turned towards his bed.

He lay down, composing himself neatly in the middle of the made-up bed and waited, knowing it would return shortly. He was ready.

And it came.

This time it was different. This time he didn't resist. This time he didn't fight back.

This time he gave himself up to the hot poker pain of the vice like cocoon as it enveloped him, coursed through him, growing tighter and hotter and tighter and hotter until he was no longer in it, but part of it.

Then it WAS him until he wasn't.

And there she was waiting.

She always had kept her promises.

The Mad Hatter

Covent Garden in London is home to the famous opera house, the old market and nowadays, to artists and entertainers who have set up camp around the market. This gentleman just screamed Mad Hatter to me with all of its — and his — outlandishness. And yes, if you look closely, that is a mouse! This was fun to write, almost fan fiction if you wish!

The Mad Hatter

It's 6 o'clock, the moons gone down and now it's time for tea
Just like it was once before with Alice and we three
The cat's gone into hiding and Alice she did flee
Leaving just the dormouse, the teapot and me.

If the Cheshire Cat were upside down
Would its grating grin be merely a frown
If the frivolous feline were dressed as a clown
Would it bounce on its head around London Town?

They claim he was stoned when he wrote about me
Why else would I smile so perpetually
And yes there's a mouse in my cup of fine tea
Why turn up my nose when it's quite plain to see?

The small mouse is white but what if it were brown
All done up in heels, tiara and long gown
Would it trip on its dress and like a rat drown
What would become of its diamonds and crown?

If while drinking my tea I swallowed mouse up
How would the mouse return to the cup
If I ask it should I sneeze, cough or hiccup
Would it look down on me for bringing it up?

Fiddle de dum and yes, fiddle de dee
You're right, this is nonsense, just jabberwocky!

Zeus Returns
The Final World Tour

This is a pretty unabashed rant that my friend Sandra called "Monty Pythonesque." I don't think she meant that as a compliment! Either way, it was fun to write and makes a statement at the same time. Whether you buy into the message or not is totally your call. (But I hope you do!)

Zeus Returns - The Final World Tour

Dear Zeus

Thank you for your e-mail enquiring about our services. At Olympia Public Relations we specialize in resurrection strategies that get results, you may have heard of some of our clients!

We empathize with your plight and agree with your comments. It is tough when, as a Greek God, you've been at the top of your game, worshipped by millions, then one day you wake up and zap, you're out of vogue. What's a God to do?

Well, you're remembered down here Zeus, for being a damned fine ruler, and your gigs as the Lord of State and Life and the Father of Gods and Men, were pretty well received. However, to achieve your goal of regaining your number one ranking as The God of the Heavens and Ruler of the Sky will require a very bold initiative.

We therefore propose a dynamic approach, reprising for mankind the talents on which your reputation was built and for which you are truly legendary. It's an exciting approach that we're calling "Zeus Returns – The Final World Tour."

As the God of the Heavens, we see you creating melt downs of the Arctic and Antarctic ice masses. Droughts, where water was once plentiful, will sweep the planet, deserts will spread to claim verdant land, forest fires will flourish.

As Ruler of the Sky, no one dared challenge the authority of the mighty Zeus. Your moodiness and temper are well known. So, at your command, fearsome thunderbolts will be unleashed to express your displeasure, lightning will flash and the clouds will open and rain ceaselessly where rain never dampened the earth before.

Terrifying tsunamis, tornadoes and tempests will traverse the world. Floods famine and pestilence will pervade the planet. Crops will fail, creatures will become extinct, many of we humans will perish.

Zeus, this is an exciting initiative that will position you as a revitalized and pertinent God, one who is raising the bar and we look forward to working with you to achieve your goals.

Yours truly

P.S. We truly believe that Mankind will definitely pay close attention to your influence on global natural events and the havoc that you will be wreaking. The loss of life, disasters and devastation will present dilemmas and future implications that are certain to make The Human Race stop, think and act…
…or not!

True Love

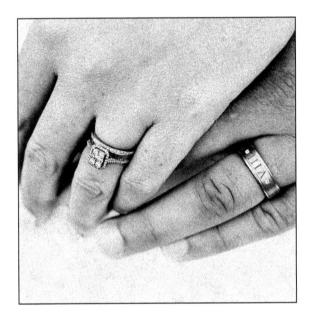

There was a story one night on the news
about the controversy that surrounds
assisted suicide. To be honest, I hadn't
really paid that much attention to the
issue but this story really struck a chord in
a way, and with a thought process, I didn't
expect. The next day I wrote 'True Love.'

True Love

You stand alongside the Doctor who stands alongside the Priest

You take a warm wet wipe and gently dab the sweat off my cheeks

You alone know that they are really tears

You ask me if I'm ready

You watch me slowly nod yes

You slide your hand over mine

You see the Doctor slide in the syringe

You close my eyes

You close your eyes

You tighten your hand around mine

You steady me as I drift towards endless sleep

You inspire my last fleeting thought

How unselfish true love can really be.

Jack 'n Jill

Originally this piece was for my 10 Commandments book that never came to fruition, so it found its home here. It deals with the theme of adultery in today's digital society, the ease with which that is possible and touches on the resulting ethical dilemmas.

Jack 'n Jill

Dan Smiley was going to have an affair with a girl he didn't know and who was about the same barely legal age as his granddaughter.

It was going to happen just over two hours from now and his wife Claire would never know.

It was his Ahmed his mechanic who'd given him the idea. Telling him over an oil change about how he'd met this woman online.

Not like a dating service, he'd said, much easier, a lot more potential for a "no strings attached" hook up and it was free.

Dan hadn't really thought anymore about the conversation till the previous week.

He'd finished losing in his online poker group, yet again, had checked out the weather and the news and was just plain old-fashioned ho-hum bored.

That's when he Googled the website Ahmed had told him about, figured out how to use it, ended up posting his ad and hooked up with her.

"I'm not gonna pay you and I'm not after cash too," she'd written after a couple of posts.

He'd told her that this wasn't the case.

"K then - let's plan it." she'd written.

And they had. His name was to be Jack. Hers Jill.

Why am I doing this, he thought. Out of boredom? Or was it to reassure himself that he still could, that he was still capable and desirable, that he had what it takes?

Yes, he thought. *All of the above.*

He hummed to himself
Jack and Jill wanted a thrill
He wasn't sure if he oughta
What the heck she said she will
She's the same age as my granddaughter
Hey, that's pretty good, he chuckled aloud.

He hadn't been looking for an eighteen year old. In fact, he'd
been mildly shocked when she connected with him.
When the idea to do this first came to him, he'd assumed it
would be with someone around his own age. Sure, he'd maybe
secretly hoped for someone younger maybe but never had
imagined it would be a kid.
What the hell will we talk about, he pondered.
I mean do I ask her how's it goin' at school for chissakes?
One part of him kept trying to get him to reject the idea, *Hey
Dan, you can always just no-show. Hell it doesn't matter.
You don't know her and she don't know you. Who cares. And
anyway, do you really need this shit in your life! Wanna live with
it after the fact?*
But the deep down Dan part found the idea compelling. It
tugged away at him on an emotional level he'd not experienced
in a very long time.
That delicious cocktail of fear, anticipation, adrenalin and lust.
Kind of like he'd felt as a schoolboy that first time with
Margaret Edwards.
He laughed to himself at the irony of it all. Forty more years of

life under his belt and here he was, back to doing a schoolgirl again.

Time to leave, he thought.

On the way down the condo hallway towards the front door his eye caught the ornately framed photograph of Claire and himself. He'd seen the picture of the two of them a thousand times but hadn't really looked at it for a while now.

He stopped. *That was one helluva fish.* He smiled, remembering the marlin they'd caught off the pier in Mazatlán. *Hell, that was a fight and a half.*

And Claire… beaming at the camera, proud as if she'd caught it herself. "Way to go Danny boy" she'd yelled. She'd called him Danny boy ever since they'd met in college.

Claire and he were what others would call content.

Complimentary, not in conflict.

A bit like an olive and a slice of lemon just floating along in that now mostly empty martini glass called marriage.

Claire's mother had called last week, whining at Claire the way she always did. "But I haven't seen you since Christmas. Can't you come for a visit. Stay a few days. Help me with some boxes?"

Claire's mother always had boxes she needed help with. To her, boxes were the magic lure that never failed to create great feelings of guilt in Claire and never failed to reel her in.

Claire had reluctantly agreed and yes, she'd stay for a few days and yes, she'd help with the damned boxes.

She'd left that morning, leaving him a long list of things to do around the house for her, and a long stretch of freedom for Dan.

"Where did the good times go?" he said to the picture.

He grabbed his keys from the hook next to the photograph, took a deep breath and opened the door.

———

Dan pulled his yellow and black F150 in behind the dump bins at the back of the restaurant parking lot.

For the first time he thought maybe he should have chosen a less flashy colour for his new truck and for some silly reason he thought about picking up a fistful of wet mud to smear over his license plate.

He leaned into the rearview mirror to check himself out.

Looking back at him he saw eyes full of apprehension, with a sheen of fear maybe, or perhaps guilt.

He squinted as he smoothed down his still full, but slightly greying hair, not bad for a guy who's just retired.

Retired – who's kidding who, he thought bitterly. He never figured that he'd be one of those guys that got a damned golden handshake.

32 years with the same company, top financial dog and the bigwigs in Japan decided they had to cut budgets, and of course, cutting budgets meant cutting people.

They'd hired a guy half his age and half his cost.

Assholes, he thought, Hope they get what's coming to them.

He paused, looking straight back into his eyes.

"Danny boy, he said softly into the mirror, "What the hell are you doing here?"

He'd pretty much convinced himself that Jill wouldn't show anyway, that she was just a kid leading him on for kicks.

He could see her now, giggling as her friends urged her on, phone in hand, replying to his post.

No, she probably wouldn't show.

He checked his watch yet again, 3.28 right on time. His eyes swept the empty parking lot.

There was an old black bike alone in a rusty rack.

She said she was eighteen . Suppose she's not and she's not legal. What then?

He was nervous as he walked towards the beat up building that was home to "The Golden Plate" restaurant, randomly realizing that he hadn't cleaned his shoes.

Don't be stupid, he laughed to himself, the mud had turned the black shoes to brown anyway.

Why you nervous? asked his conscience

Well you know. he replied consciously

Know what?

Well, nervous about what I'm doing.

You've done this before.

Yeah, but not kinda planned like this and not with an 18 year old.

How do you feel about that?

About her just being 18?

About that yes, and that this is totally premeditated, preplanned, not like the other times.

It's kind of a kick to be honest. I mean being able to screw an eighteen year old.

Like your granddaughter.

That's different, and don't bring my granddaughter into this.

Then why're you doing this?

'Cos I've got the chance to.

You're the one who made that chance, looked for it. made it happen. Why d'ya do that?

Dan was saved from answering immediately by an old shiny silver convertible coughing and spluttering to life, muffler not muffling, then backing out with tires screeching in front of him.

I think it's as much the idea, the concept as anything. The idea of being able to set up a meet to get laid with a girl you've never met. It's erotic, disgusting, intriguing, demeaning and yes, damned exciting!

———

Maria, or Jill as she was today, chained her bike to the rusty rack at the side of the restaurant. She untied her purse from the handlebars and walked around to the front door.

It was Brittany who'd had the idea originally, something she'd picked up on Facebook. A month ago there were just three playing the game but word had spread. She'd talked to Brittany and had passed her initiation a couple of weeks later. The pimply faced partner in the event couldn't believe his luck.

There were six of them now. They jokingly called the game 'The Ladder of Love.' Right now, thanks to the easy ten points for the quickie in the school library at lunch time she was on the second rung, but with the fifty points she'd get anytime now she should be able to knock that bitch Bethany off the top spot.

It felt good to be popular, to be part of a special group. Pretty soon she'd be the leader. She wasn't real keen on doing an old guy but they'd all agreed on the points system and they got a twenty five point bonus for doing a guy older than their Dad. Maria's Dad would have been forty six this year but some drunk decided to cut a couple of years off that.

Last year her Mom, moved in with the Dave guy. "Dave is now your stepdad" she declared to Maria and her younger sister. Dave seemed to think that one of his step-fatherly duties included feeling up Maria. She'd put a stop to that in a real hurry, kneeing him between the legs. Just the way her Mom had told her to do if a guy got out of hand.

That's a twist, her Mom teaching her what to do to a guy, and then the first time she'd used it was on her Mom's boyfriend. *More like step asshole,* slamming the palm of her hand on the steamed up coffee shop door and pushing it open.

She scanned the room. *Good,* she thought, *It's empty,* pretty much what she thought it would be at that time. An old slanty eyed guy looked up from behind the counter as she approached. "Iced tea with lime." she said

He fiddled and diddled behind the counter. Slid over her drink. Maria slid back a toonie and headed for a table in the corner next to the washroom.

———

Walking up to the front door of The Golden Plate it dawned on Dan that he'd been so preoccupied with the concept, the idea of what was going to happen that he'd given little thought to how it was going to happen.

He worried that around for a bit. *Sure, she'd posted that she was tired of what she called 'boys', wanted a real man, what did that*

mean? What does she expect? What does she want?
And what if he couldn't provide it. How this was going to roll
out he hadn't quite figured out yet.
Do I take the lead on this or do I leave it to her?
Shit, what about protection. He hadn't had to worry about that
before but nowadays who knows?

His gut suddenly felt like it had a squirrel in there, working out
to win Olympic gold.

And what would his Buddies think if they knew. Bruce, who
made most red-necks look positively pink, would probably hi
five him with a "way to go Danny boy".

Eric, was the sensitive kind and was super-married to his wife
and his church and would probably disown him.

I'm not gonna tell them anyway, he thought.

He peered through the glass, looking around inside. He felt a
stirring in his groin that was competing with the swirling in his
stomach for his attention.

His sweaty palm left marks on the glass door as he pushed it
open and stepped inside.

It stunk of decades of old cigarette smoke and stale fried rice.

An older oriental guy sitting at a table by the door looked up.

Dan looked over the empty tables and knew she had come. He
hadn't been sure she would.

There she was, in the corner by the washroom, sitting with her
back to the wall so she could see who walked in through the
door. Just like he was now.

―――

Yeah, that's him, must be, it's 3.30 and he's trying to look like

he's not really here.
Why do old guys always wear brown?
Brown chords, brown sweater, brown jacket.
His greying hair was probably all brown sometime.
At least he's not fat. Could have been worse.
Around 175lbs she figured, 5'9'ish, pretty good shape for his age.
A few years older than Dad would have been. Could be worse for 50 points.

———

He walked towards her. She watched him, expressionless, a plastic glass of iced tea in front of her, a crumpled half slice of lime on the table next to it.
As Dan got closer he could see she had a stud in one side of her blunt nose and a similar sized pimple on the other.
Life is about balance, the absurd thought at this time popped into his head.
But he wasn't here for her nose.
Her clean white T-shirt proclaimed 'Jesus was an Astronaut'.
Not rich. Not poor. Middle class he decided. Not a supermodel but not overweight. Dark hair. Darkish skin.
Not East Asian. Maybe Mexican.
Not tall. Not short.
Not over made up. But not careless.
He couldn't see her legs. He could see her pink and white Nikes.
Just another average schoolgirl.
Sure, just another average schoolgirl meeting an older guy to get

laid.

He pulled back the chair opposite her and shakily, slid into it. *Christ,* he thought, *this was really happening.* While in real time his mouth said "Hi, I'm Jack."

"Yes," she answered, "I'm Jill."

He was mildly surprised at the sound of her ordinary teenage girl voice. He didn't know what he'd expected.

"You came then." he said

"Yes."

"Can I get you something, another iced tea maybe?"

"No."

"How'd you get here?"

"My bike."

Her eyes hadn't left his. Her lips hadn't suggested a hint of a smile, or of pleasure.

"You're older than I thought," she said

He didn't quite know how to answer that so he didn't.

He desperately and suddenly wanted to ask her if she'd done this before.

"You done this before?"

Dan looked down and counted the grubby checkerboard tiles on the floor, waiting for her answer. He got as far as seven.

"No." she said, her brown eyes saying yes.

He cleared his throat.

"How many?"

"4 – maybe 5 now...maybe"

He just nodded.

"Why?"

"Why what?"

"Why do you do this?"

"Because I can."

Stupid as it may seem that sorta made sense

"Have you?" she asked

"No"

Her eyes stared him down.

'Well, OK, yes" feeling his face burning at being caught in the lie.

"But not like you."

"Like me?"

"You know… young."

"Pass the sugar."

He slid it over the greasy vinyl tablecloth towards her.

She slowly poured sugar into her plastic glass.

Dan waited.

"What's your real name Jack?"

"Dan,. he cleared his throat again.

"You married Dan?"

"Yeah."

She took a long sip of the iced tea.

"What would your wife think about you sitting here now?"

She stared that same blank stare.

He didn't answer.

"It doesn't really matter I guess," a first half smile curling on her lips.

She picked up her purse.

"I'm going to the washroom now – you wanna… come?"

Dan hesitated.

April Fools

I have no clue where this one came from other than my not being totally convinced around the veracity of the "good book." It just struck me that this could be the ultimate April Fools joke — and, unfortunately, the ultimate result.

April Fools

The tepid spring sun struggled through the man sized slit in the stone wall. Its weak beams cascaded across the hunched shoulders of Father Francis sitting at the worn table in the centre of the chamber.

As senior scribe to the Court of King James, translating this new version of the Holy Book had tested him in only ways that only Moses would understand.

"The King will have my head if I'm right, he'll have my head."

"But he'll also have your head if you're wrong," whispered back the second priest

"Will **you** take a look, I mean, I'm positive but it simply can't be."

"Oh no my brother, better your head than mine."

The somber faced Francis shakily laid down his quill.

Tenderly, as if grasping a newborn, he pulled the faded document towards him and squinting, began yet one more time, to read the ancient Hebrew text.

Working from right to left he precisely enunciated each syllable of each word in the passage, translating as he read it aloud…...

"… and Mo-sez ray-zed his staff and the wa-ters of the Red-Sea par-ted and the Is-rae-lites all walk-ed through. Awww…ha-ha-ha - if you bee-leeve that, I-have sum sw-amp land I-can-sell-you. This is just jib-er-ish - I made-up" he translated, "Ap-ril

Fools".

The scribe looked up, as pale as the manuscript. There **was** no doubt, **was** no mistake. He rose, moved towards the slit in the stone, pulled himself up and thrust himself outwards…. escaping forever the awful, unfathomable unspeakable truth.

"Shit!" exclaimed the second priest running to the opening. "Wait…Wait Francis…it was me! It was just for a laugh. It was all me - I did it! I dummied up the manuscript. It was just meant to be an April Fools!"

Freedom

I originally wrote this as a piece for Halloween but I kind of really liked it and didn't want to let it hang out there just for one day a year. So, I changed it up a bit so it would be broader in its appeal. I think the reason I like 'Freedom' is that in the space of a short story it encompasses many different genres of writing including the "scary" stuff that I hadn't really tried before.

Freedom

For whatever reason, the stupid cow had given him the book for his birthday a few weeks earlier. He'd tried to read the first page four times, not knowing why he even bothered.

Especially now.

'Delicate curtains and a lone cypress tree framed the milky glass that hid a life more splintered than the shingles clinging to the abandoned cabin in the glade,' he read.

"What a bunch of crap." the man snorted, "Doesn't anyone write stories you can read any more?"

He slammed the book shut and tossed it to the floor where it landed alongside the motionless, taped and tied body of his wife lying spread-eagled on the carpet.

The man sighed, eased his obese frame forward in the armchair and reached for the small Tupperware container on the coffee table next to him.

"Twenty years of hell – oh the stories I could tell," he sang softly to himself.

It was time to finish his work.

There was only one left now. John, Paul and George had already completed their mission.

The man opened the container and grasped the tweezers that lay alongside it.

The borer beetle he had lovingly named Ringo ran rapidly around the container frantically trying to avoid capture.

The man smiled as he gently gripped the beetle between the prongs of the tweezers. With great precision he placed it into the end of the plastic tube that he'd borrowed from the drinking bottle strapped to his bike.

Oh how you bugged me - now I'm bugging you, he giggled to himself.

He gently shook the tube helping Ringo twist and tumble down into the dark red wet warm folds of the left ear of his wife.

C'mon, c'mon, eat her away - just like she did to me each day.

From just above the duct tape that sealed off her mouth and nose, the woman's eyes dulled beyond pain and horror, flickered like almost spent t-lites.

Ringo crawled from the end of the tube and headed in the only direction it could, through the ragged hole of the inner ear chomped out by the three borer beetles that had gone before.

It had taken the others only a few minutes each to do their work. The man sat there waiting.

Devour her mind a bit at a time – leave it empty as she did mine.

The man sat there hating.

Then, emerging from her right ear, bloated with a belly full of brains, Ringo surfed the stream of blood as it tumbled onto the now darkly stained carpet.

Freedom thought Ringo as, sated, it struggled to its feet and scampered away.

Freedom thought the man, as his wife's unseeing eyes closed for the last time.

Freedom thought the woman, surrendering to the dark, hollow release of nothingness.

Bittersweet Beauty

There's something very special about sitting at the side of a lake at sunset. The silence can turn deafening which inspired this piece. Not sure whether it's poetry or an essay. I am sure that the mind was influenced by the moment.

Bittersweet Beauty

The exquisite symphony of sounds that signify the death of the day....

The scuffling of nocturnal creatures foraging for food, ignoring the songs of birds above as they bid farewell to the day.

The whisper of a jet plane, from six miles high, carrying the dreams and hopes of hundreds on wings and a prayer.

The lake lapping lazily to the shores, exhausted from the comings and goings of the day, carrying with it the good night calls of sleepy sounding ducks echoing across undulating waters.

Tiny winged insects dart intuitively making the most of the hiatus, their wings creating a droning back drop of white noise for the red setting sun.

The imperceptible sound of the marching boots of an army of aggressive ants who ignore the irritating whine of a distant motor craft heading home before darkness drops.

The in and out breathing of a multitude of moths, the sound of their efforts overwhelmed by a cacophony of bats swooping down on unsuspecting prey who were just trying to make a living.

The socially acceptable sound of bullfrogs burping repeatedly in the slightly swaying bullrushes that line the lake.

The faint bleating of a baby begging for more and the cooing, soothing answer of a mother who hasn't any.

The rhythmic repetition of a single indigenous drum beating a distant solo invoking the presence of good spirits to bring a safe night.

The sound of a nearby drum answering, its swelling, bursting percussive crescendo filling my ears.

The realization too late that this exploding drum was deep inside me, was me.

I now know that as the sun sets it also rises in another place, in another time, bringing with it the dawning of delicious understanding.

Bittersweet beauty.

No Fool Mary

A Christmas story that I wrote, tongue in cheek, to provoke a reaction from my wife. For whatever reason, she is convinced that I believe that Jesus was actually an astronaut. Needless to say, this is contrary to her theological thinking!

No Fool Mary

The interplanetary flying machine sliced across the night sky, a fiery chariot as it entered the atmosphere of the 3rd planet that circled the 9th sun from home.

"So this is it," said the woman, "Then it's time."

"Yes," replied her partner swiftly stabbing out the blue flashing light on the screen, "It's time."

The light stopped flashing. Outside, the shields slid up silently. An aura of white light, brighter than any star, enveloped the chariot which floated still and suspended in the northern sky.

The woman sighed, "I will get him now."

Carrying a baby, the woman stepped into the chamber. Her partner followed. The door hissed as it closed. The energy field absorbed them.

"We did it to ourselves didn't we?" the woman spoke softly as she activated the download transporter.

"We didn't know any better until it was too late." replied her partner.

"But the signs were all there. Dramatically changing weather patterns, natural upheaval everywhere, disappearing species…"

"…and then Armageddon."

"Yes, we were lucky to get away."

"The baby, he's the last you know."

"I know."

They materialized outside of a shack. A few cattle and donkeys were grazing from a rickety feeding trough nearby.

The woman's partner stepped forward and with great resolve, rapped upon the door.

Inside, old Joe, whose amorous advances were yet again being fended off by his wife and who had yet to consummate his recent marriage, rolled over and cursed.

"Who in the heavens can that be at this time?"

Getting up, he pulled on his pants and pulled open the door.

"We have brought you the future of mankind." the woman announced gravely.

"Huh?" questioned Joe blankly.

"Who is it Joe?" shouted Mary, quite relieved with the interruption in the proceedings.

"We have brought you a baby. He is the last and he is the first." continued the woman

Mary, overhearing this shouted, "Hey, let 'em in Joe and put the baby out in the manger with the animals for now, it's warmer in the hay."

Joe took the baby and headed towards the manger.

"Come in, come on in," she welcomed the strangers, "Where did you say you were from?"

Mary smiled to herself, *Hallelujah, it's a miracle*, she thought, *this could work out really quite well. All of the glory, none of the grunge!*

My Lady of the Lake

This fantasy was totally inspired by this
wonderful image by a photographer friend of
mine, Carolyn Haggart. As soon as I saw the
photograph the storyline leaped into my mind.

My Lady Of The Lake

For almost three summers we had met this way.
Me, skipping stones into the limpid lake on a lazy Sunday
afternoon.
She, emerging from the water - sensuous serene, silent.
My Lady of the Lake.
She never spoke.

I began to talk to her, sharing secrets, rants, ramblings and
meandering monologues.
I'd tell her of my childhood, what it was like growing up with
my family.
I'd share memories of my schooldays, of being taught, of
learning life's lessons.
Of breaking rules and breaking hearts.
She never spoke.

I'd tell her of my teenage years, what it was like growing up
without my family.
I'd speak of hopes that were just hype and of promises
postponed.
Of wanting something more but not knowing what more was.
She never spoke.

I'd tell her of falling in love soon after marrying somebody else.
Of the fear of looking into the frumpled, forgiving face of my firstborn.
Of learning the power of compromise and the peace of contentment.
She never spoke.

And so it went on. Me sharing my stories while skipping stones.
She silent, stone faced unmoving, listening.
That final Sunday, I made my way through the waving grasses to our own private nook on the shore of the lake. I bent over and gathered my usual handful of stones.
I stopped. I stood up. There she was on the shore. Waiting for me.
This had never happened before.
I was confused.

I stepped towards her my mouth forming unknown words.
And for the very first time, my Lady of the Lake spoke.
"Where is Arthur?" she said, "And what of Excalibur?"

The Letter

The Letter is another work inspired by a writing prompt. It's a powerful fictional poem/story that is a letter from a father to a son that have never met each other — and now, never will. This was difficult to write as there's shades of me in there somewhere. I'm glad I persevered and got it out.

The Letter

You don't know me and I don't know you
Your mother was a whore mongering tramp
But I guess I was too
You know the truth is, I don't even know if you're mine
I always took the blame anyway.
You look like me a bit I wonder
I think that I kinda hope so
You've maybe got yourself your own son by now
Perhaps he looks like me too, maybe
I hope you get what I didn't.
You get to change the kid's diaper
You get choked up the first time he looks back, waving shyly as
he walks into the schoolyard
You get to lace up his smelly, second hand skates
You get to wish you were young again when he brings home his
first girl
You get to see him married, proper like.
You get to watch him do what needs to be done to feed his
family
You get to see him make mistakes – then figure things out and
get them right
You get to feel the thrill of him doing something a damn sight
better than anyone else

You get to tell him not to let his emotions over-rule his common sense

You don't let him be me…oh no, don't let him be me

I've got a few more days the Doc says

I thought whoever, whatever and wherever you are

You might wanna know. But…

You don't need to feel bad for me 'cos…

I don't know you and you don't know me.

Skin

As any author will tell you most stories never come out the way they were planned. 'Skin' is a great example of that. It started as a poem examining the texture of skin and relating that to the texture of life. But no, that would have been too easy! Somehow I shot off on the tangent that became the story here. I'm glad I followed my nose, I like the piece a lot.

Skin

I twirl random strands of her fine black hair between my still trembling fingers and thumb.

It's damp.

Liquid afterglow, I think idly, gazing up at my great-grandmother's chandelier hoping that she wasn't gazing down right now.

I turn, raise my head, punch the pillow and settle in closer.

"Have you ever kissed a moose?" I whisper to her

Her chest heaves against mine as she laughs. A full-on Lauren Bacall laugh.

"No, serious, I mean really kissed a moose, like right on the lips?"

"Are you kidding me. ARE YOU KIDDING ME!" She heaves herself up on one elbow and looks down at me, frowning.

"Hey, just 'cos I got some Metis blood in me you think I go 'round kissing moose, have you ever been even **close** to one of those big ugly suckers?"

Smiling, she flicks her finger against the end of my nose in mocking rebuke.

I flick her nose in return. She laughs that laugh again and returns to her rightful place.

Next to me.

We lie together. Comfortable. Close. Satisfied. Silent.

Thinking perhaps about what just was. Or, maybe of what could be.

I know I am.

What an idiotic thing to say, I think, angry with....NO, not angry – **annoyed** with myself.

I mean, kissing a moose, where the hell did that come from.

I could have, should have, I **meant** to say something caring, kind. I dunno, something NICE for chissakes.

But no. That's me. Always have to be the comedian.

I guess to be honest I was maybe a bit scared, confused even, not just about what to say but what to THINK!.

She, and this, it's all new.

She's purring now. The soft sweet snoring of contentment.

Her breath warms my skin.

I lie here just looking at her.

Not **seeing** her. Just looking at her.

I don't yet know her enough to **see** her.

Funny huh.

Funny how we share our bodies more willingly than we share what we think, or who we are.

I guess I'll settle for that for now.

She stirs, squirms and shifts her body next to mine.

Half asleep, half awake, she reaches out and gently slides the back of her finger nails across the still moist skin of my breast.

I shudder.

"I really like you Sarah. I like you a lot," she murmurs.

The Folks Who Live By Our Pond

Living on 20 acres in the woods, with a huge natural pond, always meant there were plenty of photo opportunities, so I often took my camera with me when walking the land. On passing by the pond one afternoon I literally stopped in my tracks. There was what I thought was a small crowd of older folks hanging out by my pond — except, they weren't people, they were bulrushes! What a great photo op. and naturally, a subsequent piece of writing!

The Folks Who Live By Our Pond

They are the folks who live by our pond.

They are infinitely superior to us.

They bob and sway seemingly burdened by the knowledge of time.

They survey their surroundings with a superior, sorrowful gaze, standing tall, pitying their neighbours, those who are lesser than they.

They are omnipotent, condescendingly, grudgingly sharing private pearls of wisdom amongst one another.

They are stately in the sadness and frustration of their mute imprisonment.

They are wise beyond their years.

They know the intimate secrets of the forest.

They know why deer chose particular and proven paths.

They know where the muskrat makes her mansion.

They know precisely when the great blue heron will visit, perusing the pond for its supper.

They know the hidden gathering places of the slippery speckled trout.

They know that as the storm clouds gather, when the rain pelts and pounds they must withdraw within themselves.

They understand that as the seasons change then so must they.
They wait stoically, knowing that as time passes, as they grow
more fragile, the winds and the birds will feast relentlessly on
what was their impeccable majesty.

They are forlornly patient, knowing their demise is an
inevitability.

They quietly accept that from their seed will be born new
keepers of the knowledge, who in turn will be known as…

The folks who live by our pond.

Not Your Tide Pods

This is a straight up Halloween story with a bit of a twist at the end. It was written for a contest with my local Writers' Club and was simply a lot of fun to write.

Not Your Tide Pods

Bursts of laughter floated through the darkening dusk as the three Dads tossed back their heads, tossed back their beers and stopped outside the biggest house on the block.

Two princesses, Superman and a rather worse for wear werewolf scampered up the driveway towards the front door, ducking under the 8ft wide black hairy spider hanging from a tree branch. Their plastic grocery bags already bulging with their take for the night.

"Trick or treat" they shrieked, their flushed faces the colour of vampire blood.

There was no answer.

"Trick or treat" they tried again with somewhat less enthusiasm than before.

Still no answer.

"Hey kids – let's go," called out one of the Dads.

The quartet turned and shuffled towards the waiting beer drinkers.

"Anyone want my popcorn?" asked Superman, "I'll trade ya."

"I'll trade you my Bubblicious if you want," said one of the princesses.

"No, I want the Bubblicious," whined the werewolf.

"Get lost," his sister the princess shot at him.

"How many you got?" asked Superman.

"I got…" she paused as she fumbled around in the bag,
"I got six but I'll only trade you….."

That's when the werewolf screamed.
Yellowish rancid smelling gel like pods, filled with pus, had begun to vomit violently from the end of each of the spider's eight hairy legs.
The noise was like hail on the roof of a cheap import van as by the hundreds of thousands they splattered on to the driveway, the pods splitting as they hit.
Myriad miniature convulsing, hairy legged spiders spewed out turning the grey concrete to asphalt black.
Hungrily they swarmed over four pairs of little feet, crunching and munching through rubber, plastic and leather footwear, devouring young tender skin, bones and flesh.
Blood gushed down the driveway towards three shocked immobile fathers. An abandoned beer can bobbed along swept away on the red wave.

"Cut," yelled the Director. "More blood – I want more blood. This piece of crap they call a movie has at least gotta look real." he sighed in exasperation.
"OK people, let's take a break, give me more blood for chrissakes and we'll do another take."
That's when he felt the white hot pain of thousands of incessant pin pricks attacking his left foot and looking down, he saw the red blood streaming from the stub at the end of his leg.

The Empathetic Doe

This was written to celebrate the Winter Games held recently in the town in which I live. Deer roam the trails near my home and I wondered what they would think of it all! I like the emotion of the animal responding to the human struggle and pain in this piece.

The Empathetic Doe

The cumulous clouds clustered and formed a graceful arc over the distant hills.

The wind awoke and whipped across the flatlands warming as it went on its way.

A pearl of ice slipped from a twig delicately splashing the tip of her wrinkled, frozen nose as she bit down on an equally wrinkled frozen berry.

She twitched her nostrils, switched the angle of her head and slid the shrivelled sweet treat on to her tongue.

Her body stiffened nervously, feeling the vibration of the ground.

Getting stronger now.

Her ears perked. Her body now rigid, quivering.

Pronghorns she thought feeling thundering hooves.

Getting closer now.

She backed away from the trail into the bush, eyes darting, head sweeping, searching for the source of the soundless charge.

She heard them now. No, not pronghorns. Humans. They were noisier, clumsier than pronghorns, with long feet that made a swishing sound as they slid through the chinook slush and snow.

She saw them now. Moving faster than she'd ever seen them move before.

One after another in single file.

She stood silently, unmoving as they came toward her.

She could hear the panting, the gruff sounds of exertion as they passed by, oh so closely, on their important journey.

Her eyes watched their eyes. All were unwavering, focused, determined.

And still they came. Swish. Swish. Swish. Swish.

A straggler was about to pass, panting heavier than the others she thought, breathing in hard and hardly breathing out. She caught his words of hope, of determination, of prayer.

"Dear God - I CAN do this – I KNOW I can do this – please let me finish God – I can DO this – I'll promise you anything but PLEASE let me…." The voice faded as the straggler disappeared around a bend in the trail.

The young doe hung her head. Her heart going out to the human. A pearl of a tear delicately splashed the tip of her wrinkled, frozen nose.

My Underwood

Those of a certain age will know what an Underwood is. And for those who don't know what a typewriter is, well, this memoir moment will be lost on you so go Google it!

My Underwood

Some 30 years after Italian composer Rossini wrote The William Tell Overture an American named John T. Underwood produced the first typewriter bearing his name.

It's a pretty fair guess that neither of these esteemed gentlemen ever suspected that in a different century their respective talents would align and have a significant influence on a young man named Martin Povey.

Up to the age of fourteen being a student in the UK meant following a general educational process - a bit like the grade system in North America. On reaching fourteen, the system (back then) gave me choices in terms of what type of a schooling I wanted to continue with. I could choose from three different streams

1. An enriched general educational stream that was typically for the smart kids preparing them for University or College
2. A technical stream which included metalwork, woodwork, drafting etc., this was to prepare the boys for the workplace, usually in the trades
3. A stream called commercial, which included bookkeeping, typing, home economics etc., this was primarily for girls, to prepare them for roles deemed appropriate for the fairer sex back then.

So, what's a hormone hopping 14 year old to do? Well, I wasn't that smart, I had no interest in guy kinda stuff but I did have a great interest in girls! It was a no brainer and thinking back I really can't remember my parent's reaction to my decision. Anyway, suffice to say that I spent the next two years in a classroom with twenty nine girls.

Enter Miss Matthews, our typing teacher, a bespectacled, spinsterish woman to offensively typecast her, (pun just realized on re-reading) who to me at that time seemed to be a hundred years old!

But Miss Matthews had two huge assets going for her. One she had the patience of Job and two, she had a pile of 78 records. The patience was learned and the 78s were to teach.

In the beginning, on would go record #1 of The William Tell Overture, a very slow version, and thirty sets of fingers would faithfully follow the rhythms of the music slowly tapping out our typing exercises on our Underwood typewriters. Then record by record the pace picked up until by record # 5 we had reached the breathtaking speed of maybe thirty words a minute.

Class by class, record by record, semester by semester, faster and faster went The William Tell Overture and eighteen months later, with a mind of their own, fingers flew frantically across the Underwood keyboard to the record #10 of 10. By exam time, according to Miss Matthews and her ever present stop watch, I clocked in at a very respectable seventy two words a minute.

For most people of a certain age the sound of the William Tell Overture brings back memories of the Lone Ranger, Tonto and "hi ho silver". But for me, each time I hear that piece I can't help but think of Miss Matthews, a quick brown fox, my twenty nine girlfriends and of course, my trusty Underwood.

:defghijklmnopqrstuvwxyz ABCDEFGHIJKLMNOPQRSTUVWXYZ
:4567890.:;' " (!?) +-*/=

The quick brown fox jumps over the lazy dog. 123456'

The quick brown fox jumps over th

The quick brown fox jumps

The quick brown 1

The quick bro

The quick

The quic

The Ferris Wheel

The Ferris Wheel, or any fairground ride for that matter, means loud music and the screams of teenage girls. I couldn't resist writing this as, to me, the photograph exudes exactly that. And why do they scream anyway?

The Ferris Wheel

Jody's stomach lurched as she looked up from her seat at the Ferris wheel looming above her. She picked at her nose nervously, preferring the left nostril.

She smoothed down her favourite skimpy, salmon skirt that had just blown up over her polka dot panties bought privately on line especially for this occasion.

Jody was ready. She closed her eyes in anticipation.

Lightheaded, and slightly fearful, she reached for the hand of her best friend Marcie sitting next to her. Marcie gripped her friend's moist and warm hand, squeezing it tightly as the Ferris wheel began its three minute voyage to heaven and back.

Jody felt her body trembling as it remembered when, earlier that summer, it had unexpectedly felt the pulsing thrill for the first time. The ride picked up speed.

Jody's breathing now urgent, her heart pounding as she, Marcie and the ride rocked and rolled in rhythm with the heavy metal music blasting out from below, filling her head and filling the skies.

Eyes still closed, she flung back her head and let out the much anticipated scream, her whole body shuddering as both the Ferris wheel and Jody reached their climax.

And time froze. Coming down now.... shaking...

slowing....stopping.

Jody, legs shivering and weak, held on to Marcie's shoulder as the two girls clambered unsteadily out of the compartment.

Marcie turned, leaned forward and gave Jody a quick hug, whispering "Way to go girl."

Giggling, they made their way back to where Jody's pimply faced boyfriend was tossing back the last of an illegal beer.

"Want to go again?" he smirked.

Jody just smiled.

Martin and Mary Lou share a laugh together

A Note from The Author

Thanks for choosing to read *Write Out of My Mind,* I hope you had as many positive diverse thoughts and reactions reading it as I had writing it!

If you have any comments, questions or nice things to say about the book then I'd love to hear from you. You can always reach me through my website at martinpovey.net.

Write Out of My Mind is available in Paperback or as an E-Book through Amazon, Blurb.com, Apple Ibooks Store and many leading retailers. It's also available through my website at martinpovey.net.

You can also join my mailing list on my website at martinpovey.net and I'll keep you up to date on special events, appearances, promotions and exciting news about a couple of upcoming projects.

My thanks again and here's to your reading pleasure!

Martin Povey

CPSIA information can be obtained
at www.ICGtesting.com
Printed in the USA
FFHW011555210319
51141397-56605FF